For Gemk,

Whose endless supply of ideas and honest critique made this possible.

感謝 Gemk

源源不絕的靈感及誠懇的建議讓這一切成真。

The Rebel Rabbit
離家出走！

Coleen Reddy 著

馮馭、蔡宏 繪

薛慧儀 譯

三民書局

Robert Rabbit didn't like being young, because when you're young,
you have to listen to all the older rabbits that just love telling you what to do.
He had to listen to his parents,

his grandparents

and his teachers.

小兔羅伯特一點都不喜歡當隻小兔子，
因為只要你還小，就得聽所有長輩的話，
而且他們最愛叫你做這個做那個的；
羅伯特得聽爸爸、媽媽、爺爺、奶奶還有老師們的話。

One day, he was going out to play a game of rugby when his mother called him.

"What?" he yelled.

"Come here right now, young rabbit. You're not going anywhere until you clean up your room," said his mother.

4

有一天，他正想要出去玩橄欖球的時候，被媽媽叫住了。
「做什麼啦？」他喊著。
「小兔子，馬上給我過來！沒把你的房間整理好之前，
哪兒都不准去！」媽媽說。

Robert went to his room. He was really angry.
Why should he clean his room? He liked it better when it was dirty.
He was tired of listening to his parents.
He decided to rebel.

羅伯特走回房間，他好生氣喔！
為什麼他該整理房間呢？
他比較喜歡房間亂亂的樣子嘛！
他再也不想聽爸媽的話了。
他決定要做個壞小孩。

He would run away and do what he liked.
He would play rugby all day and **never** have to clean his room
or do his homework or take a bath.
He packed his bag with his comic books and climbed out of the window.

　　他要跑得遠遠的，做自己喜歡的事。
他可以整天玩橄欖球，再也不必整理房間、寫功課，也不用洗澡了！
　　於是他把漫畫書放進背包裡，從窗戶爬了出去。

He met his friends at the park and played rugby all day.
When it started getting dark, all his friends wanted to go home.
"Don't go home. Stay and play rugby with me," pleaded Robert.

他在公園遇見朋友，
玩了一整天的橄欖球。
天色開始變暗，朋友們全都要回家了。
「別回家嘛！留下來和我玩橄欖球嘛！」羅伯特懇求著。

11

"We're hungry. We have to go home before our mothers get angry!
You have to go home too," said his friends.
"No, I don't have to go home anymore. I am a rebel. I have run away
from home. Why don't you join me and then we can all stay and play
rugby?" asked Robert, his face lighting up.

"We'd rather eat dinner," said his friends and they all went home.

「我們肚子餓了呀！我們得在媽媽生氣前
趕緊回家才行。你也該回家了呀！」朋友們說。
「才不呢！我再也不必回家了。我是個壞小孩，我已經離家出走了！
你們也可以加入我的行列，那我們就可以整天留在這裡玩橄欖球了呀！」
羅伯特說著說著，整張小臉都亮了起來。

「我們寧願回家吃晚餐。」他的朋友們全都回家去了。

Robert the rabbit was all alone in the park.
Running away from home so that he could play rugby all the
time seemed like a stupid idea if there was no one to play with.
"I'll just go on my way," thought Robert to himself as he started walking.

小兔羅伯特孤伶伶地留在公園裡。
如果沒有人可以陪他一起玩，那麼為了能
整天玩橄欖球而離家出走，似乎只是個笨主意。
「我自己走好了！」羅伯特這樣想著，開始在路上遊蕩。

After some time, Robert got really hungry.

He passed some houses and he could smell food.

He had no money to buy food.

He thought of stealing food, but if he got caught,

he would be taken back to his parents.

過了一會兒，羅伯特的肚子好餓好餓。
他經過幾棟屋子，聞到食物香噴噴的味道。
但是他身上沒有錢買東西吃。
他想過要去偷點食物，可是如果被抓了，
他就會被帶回去交給他爸爸媽媽了。

Robert found a bench and fell asleep.

He wasn't asleep for long before he was pushed off the bench.

He opened his eyes and saw a raccoon.

"This is MY bench!" yelled the raccoon.

羅伯特找到一張長凳，
躺在上頭睡著了。
才睡了一會兒，他就被推了下來！
他張開眼睛一看，是一隻浣熊。
「這是我的凳子！」浣熊大聲嚷著。

19

Robert began to think about home.

Without doing much he got a bed to sleep in and food to eat.

If he ran away, how would he get those things?

羅伯特這下子開始想家了。

在家裡，他不用做什麼，就有床可以睡，有東西可以吃。

如果他離家出走了，他要怎樣才能得到這些東西呢？

Robert thought about going home.
His parents were probably sick with worry.
He could picture them crying and wishing
they hadn't been so mean to him.
Maybe they had learned their lesson.
He decided to go home.

羅伯特想回家了。
說不定爸爸媽媽現在正擔心得要命呢！
他可以想像他們哭泣的模樣，並希望自己
以前沒有對他這麼兇就好了。
也許他們已經學到教訓了呢！
於是他決定回家了。

When he got to his house, everything was very quiet.
Robert was expecting his parents to be crying.
"Maybe they're in shock," thought Robert happily as
he climbed back into his room through the window.

當他回到家時，屋子裡非常安靜。
羅伯特原本以為爸爸媽媽會在哭泣的。
「說不定他們驚嚇過度昏倒了。」羅伯特高興地想著，
一面從窗戶爬進自己的房間裡。

There was no one in his room.

He could hear voices downstairs.

Then he heard a loud noise.

"They're crying, they're crying,"

Robert thought with a smile and went downstairs.

房間裡一個人也沒有，
樓下倒是有一些聲音，
接著又聽到很大的噪音。
「他們在哭呢！他們在哭呢！」
羅伯特想著，臉上掛著笑容跑下樓去。

But as he got nearer, he realized that his parents were laughing.

His dad was telling his mom a joke!

They were happy that he was gone.

Robert was about to run away again when his mother saw him.

28

他走近一點，才發現爸爸媽媽是在笑！
爸爸正在說一個笑話給媽媽聽。
羅伯特不在家，他們還很高興的樣子呢！
羅伯特正想再一次跑走時，媽媽看見他了。

"Have you finally finished cleaning your room now?" asked his mother
with a smile. "How about some dinner?"
They didn't even know that he had become
a rebel and run away!
That was fine with Robert! He was hungry!
"Sure," said Robert and he sat down
to eat dinner with his family.

「你房間到底整理完了沒有呀？」媽媽笑著問：「要不要吃點晚餐呀？」
他們根本不知道羅伯特曾經變成一個壞孩子，還離家出走了呢！
沒關係！這樣也好，而且他餓壞了。
「當然好囉！」羅伯特說，然後坐下來和爸爸媽媽一起吃晚餐。

糟糕!小兔子羅伯特出去探險,
結果竟然迷路了!聰明的小朋友,
快來幫小兔子羅伯特找到回家的路吧!

33

生字表

 p. 4

rugby [`rʌgbɪ] 名 橄欖球

yell [jɛl] 動 大聲喊叫

 p. 6

rebel [rɪ`bɛl] 動 反叛
　　　　[`rɛbḷ] 名 叛徒；反抗者

 p. 10

plead [plid] 動 懇求

 p. 18

raccoon [ræ`kun] 名 浣熊

 p. 22

picture [`pɪktʃɚ] 動 想像
mean [min] 形 惡劣的

 p. 24

shock [ʃɑk] 名 震驚

你找到路了嗎？
這就是回家的路哦！

全新創作 英文讀本
帶給你優格（yogurt）般，青春的酸甜滋味！

Teens' Chronicles

愛閱雙語叢書

青春記事簿

大維的驚奇派對／秀寶貝，說故事／杰生的大秘密
傑克的戀愛初體驗／誰是他爸爸？
叛逆大維打工記／外星老師來上課／耶！放假了！

你我身上純真的影子，
透過一篇篇幽默風趣的故事重現，
推薦你這套青春無悔的創作系列，
讓愛玫、杰生、大維、凱爾、海倫、傑克，
帶你進入他們的世界，品味另一種學習英語的全新感受。

國家圖書館出版品預行編目資料

The Rebel Rabbit:離家出走! / Coleen Reddy著;馮
馭, 蔡宏繪; 薛慧儀譯.－－初版一刷.－－臺北
市; 三民, 2003
　　面; 公分－－(愛閱雙語叢書.二十六個妙朋
友系列) 中英對照
ISBN 957-14-3761-1 (精裝)

1.英國語言－讀本

523.38　　　　　　　　　　　　　92008824

© **The Rebel Rabbit**
——離家出走!

著作人　Coleen Reddy
繪　圖　馮馭 蔡宏
譯　者　薛慧儀
發行人　劉振強
著作財
產權人　三民書局股份有限公司
　　　　臺北市復興北路386號
發行所　三民書局股份有限公司
　　　　地址／臺北市復興北路386號
　　　　電話／(02)25006600
　　　　郵撥／0009998-5
印刷所　三民書局股份有限公司
門市部　復北店／臺北市復興北路386號
　　　　重南店／臺北市重慶南路一段61號
初版一刷　2003年7月
　編　號　S 85651-1
　定　價　新臺幣壹佰捌拾元整
行政院新聞局登記證局版臺業字第○二○○號

ISBN　957-14-3761-1　(精裝)